Measuring Time

Times of the Day

Tracey Steffora

Heinemann Library
Chicago, Illinois

www.heinemannraintree.com
Visit our website to find out
more information about
Heinemann-Raintree books.

To order:
☎ Phone 888-454-2279
▣ Visit www.heinemannraintree.com
to browse our catalog and order online.

Edited by Tracey Steffora and Dan Nunn
Designed by Richard Parker
Picture research by Hannah Taylor
Originated by Capstone Global Library Ltd
Printed and bound in the United States of America,
North Mankato, MN

14 13 12 11 10
10 9 8 7 6 5 4 3 2 1

Library of Congress Cataloging-in-Publication Data
Steffora, Tracey.
 Times of the day / Tracey Steffora.
   p. cm.—(Measuring time)
Includes bibliographical references and index.
 ISBN 978-1-4329-4903-7 (hc)—ISBN 978-1-4329-4910-5 (pb) 1.
Time—Juvenile literature. 2. Day—Juvenile
literature. 3. Time measurement—Juvenile literature. I. Title.
 QB209.5.S748 2011
 529'.1—dc22
              2010028872

Acknowledgments
We would like to thank the following for permission to reproduce
photographs: Alamy Images pp. **7** (©blickwinkel), **8** (©Aurora
Photos), **12** (©MBI), **14** (©Kirk Treakle), **20** (©Inspirestock Inc.);
Photolibrary pp. **4** (Comstock), **10** (Image Source), **11** (Corbis), ,
17 (Image Source), **18** (Aflo Foto Agency/Masakazu Watanabe),
19 (Radius Images); istockphoto pp. **16** ©Ana Abejon, **22**
©Bartosz Hadyniak; shutterstock pp. **5** (©Yarygin), **6** (©Kushch
Dmitry), **9** (©Martin Fowler), **13** (©oriontrail), **15** (©Multiart),
21 (©Leagam), **23 top** (©oriontrail), **23 bot** (©Damian Gil).

Front cover photograph of boy in bed reproduced with
permission of Photolibrary (Flirt Collection/Randy Faris). Back
cover photograph of students eating lunch reproduced with
permission of Alamy Images (© MBI).

Every effort has been made to contact copyright holders of
any material reproduced in this book. Any omissions will
be rectified in subsequent printings if notice is given to
the publisher.

Contents

What Is Time?

Time is how long something takes.

Time is when things happen.

There is daylight and darkness in each day.

We look and listen to know what
time of day it is.

Morning

Morning is the first part of the day.

Birds sing in the morning.

The Sun rises in the morning.

We eat breakfast in the morning.

We go to school or work in
the morning.

Noon

Noon is the middle of the day.

The Sun is high in the sky at noon.

We eat lunch in the middle of the day.

A clock reads 12:00 at noon.

Afternoon

In the afternoon we go home from school.

In the afternoon we play with friends.

Evening

Evening is the end of the day.

The Sun sets in the sky in the evening.

We eat dinner in the evening.

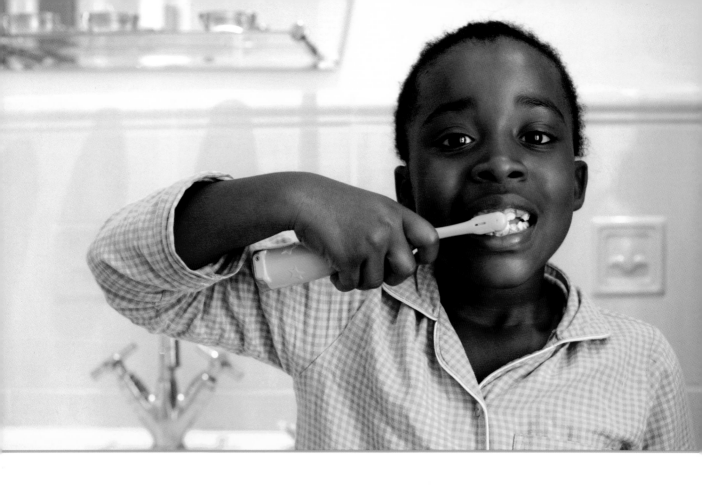

We get ready for bed in the evening.

Night

At night the sky is dark.

We sleep and dream at night.

A New Day

In the morning we wake up and start a new day! What will you do today?

Picture Glossary

daylight sunlight, or light during the day

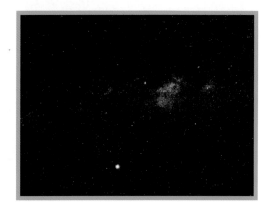

darkness little or no light

Index

Note to Parents and Teachers

Before reading

Gather pictures of daily events, such as meals, nap, playtime, and bedtime. Ask children to describe what is happening. Then ask them to pick out the photo that shows what happens first each day. Ask them to choose what happens next, and so on. This activity helps children use time words as well as place events in a logical sequence.

After reading

- Review the times of day and discuss with children clues that help them know the time of day (e.g., clocks, bells, sunlight, hunger, tiredness, and other sounds or activities that happen at consistent times of the day).
- If children are ready, explain day and night using a globe to represent the Earth and a flashlight to represent the Sun. Find your location on the globe and explain that the Earth makes a full rotation every 24 hours. Model how we experience day and night by slowly spinning the globe as a child acts as the "Sun" and holds the flashlight.